For Finley Rae Hahn

ORCHARD BOOKS

First published in 2016 in the United States by Little, Brown and Company
First published in Great Britain in 2017 by The Watts Publishing Group

1 3 5 7 9 10 8 6 4 2

HASBRO and its logo, BLYTHE, LITTLEST PET SHOP, and all related characters are
trademarks of Hasbro and are used with permission.

© 2017 Hasbro. All Rights Reserved.

A CIP catalogue record for this book is available from the British Library.

ISBN 978 1 40834 456 9

Printed in Great Britain

The paper and board used in this book are made from wood from responsible sources

Orchard Books
An imprint of Hachette Children's Group
Part of The Watts Publishing Group Limited
Carmelite House, 50 Victoria Embankment, London EC4Y 0DZ

An Hachette UK Company

www.hachette.co.uk
www.hachettechildrens.co.uk

Panda-Monium!
Starring Penny Ling

Written by Lisa Shea

ORCHARD

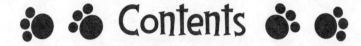 # Contents

Chapter 1
Pet Shop Post

"Minka, stop fidgeting," Blythe said to the cute pink spider monkey. "The Pet Pageant is only two weeks away, and I need to finish your outfit, plus all the others."

"I know, Blythe! But I'm just so excited about the pageant! And I love my new outfit!" Minka suddenly jumped away from Blythe to look at herself in a full-length mirror. "Oh, Blythe, it's just beautiful."

"It did turn out pretty well," Blythe agreed. Blythe's creation was a sky-blue sundress with straps that criss-crossed the back.

Minka gave Blythe a hug. "You're the best designer in the whole world!" she cried.

"And you're the sweetest spider monkey," Blythe replied.

Ring-a-ling!

Everyone in the pet store turned to see who was at the door. It was Lewis, the postman, with a parcel for Blythe. He looked at Minka and Blythe hugging.

"I've always read that monkeys are very affectionate creatures," he said. "I guess it's true."

"Oh, it's true all right," Blythe answered, with a quick glance at Minka telling her to keep quiet. Blythe had a big secret – she could communicate with animals. While other people just heard barks, squawks, growls, chirps and meows, Blythe heard actual words. At first, Blythe found her ability a little scary, but now she wouldn't change things for the world.

Blythe looked at the parcel. "Oh, this must be the special fabric I ordered," she said.

Just at that moment, Zoe came running over to Blythe. "Did I hear you say 'special fabric'?" she asked. The Cavalier King Charles spaniel started pawing the

parcel curiously.

Lewis couldn't hear what she said, of course. All he heard was a dog yapping excitedly. "Well! Isn't she a nosy little thing? You'd almost think she knew what was in that!"

"Almost," Blythe agreed. She waited until Lewis was gone to open the parcel and take out the beautiful fabrics.

Zoe sighed as she gazed at the bolts of soft silk and shiny satin.

"Don't worry, Zoe," Blythe assured her. "Even though you can't enter the Pet Pageant this year, I'm going to make you a new outfit, too."

Zoe gave a little pout. "Tell me again – why can't I enter?"

"Because you won last year," Blythe reminded her. "And were runner-up the year before. The judges decided it wasn't

fair to the other pets," she
said gently.

"I guess I can
understand that," Zoe
said as she admired her
reflection in a mirror. She
looked around. "We certainly have a
lot of possible winners here," she said.
"Since I can't compete this time, maybe
I'll give them tips on poise, beauty and
talent."

"That would be awesome," Blythe
told her. "You're the most poised and
glamorous pet I know!"

"Me too!" Zoe agreed, her eyes
sparkling with excitement. "I can't wait
to turn these pets into pageant stars!"

Chapter 2
I Pick Penny!

Blythe decided to take the pets to the beach. As they were all frolicking, Zoe rushed over to Blythe. "Guess who's entering the Perfect Pet Pageant!" she squealed. Before Blythe could answer, Zoe held up a phone. "Kitty Velvet!" she said dramatically.

Russell and Sunil came over. "Who's Kitty Velvet?" Sunil asked.

"Who's Kitty Velvet? She's the most gorgeous feline on the face of the Earth!" Zoe showed the pets photos of a beautiful black cat with a dramatic white stripe down her back. "OK. In order to compete against Kitty, you are definitely going to need my help." Suddenly, her eyes lit on Penny Ling, who was playing frisbee on the beach with Pepper. Penny was panting as she chased after the frisbee; pandas weren't used to running!

"Penny, I choose you," Zoe said dramatically. "I will be your mentor for the Perfect Pet Pageant! I think you have a lot of potential, but you need help with poise and grooming. I'm going to make you a *star*!"

Zoe was surprised when Penny was

silent. Penny didn't know if she really wanted to compete in a pageant – much less be a star!

"Let Zoe coach you," Pepper said. "All of us will still be in the contest because it will be fun, but we'll all try to help you win!"

Penny still hesitated.

"I'll make you an extra-special outfit," Blythe told her. "I know you don't like a lot of fuss, but I'll make you something very simple and elegant."

"I'm not very good at being the centre of attention," Penny said.

"That's what I'm here for!" Zoe said.

After a bit more humming and hawing,

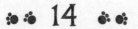

Penny grudgingly agreed to enter the pageant.

After all, Penny thought, *Zoe does know all about modelling and performing. How hard can being in a pageant be?*

Chapter 3
Pageant Prep

Penny dreamed she was on a beautiful white sandy beach. The water was sparkling, and she was eating a big bowl of bamboo shoots. The lapping waves seemed to be calling her name. *Penny … Pennnnnyyyyyy!*

"PENNY!"

Penny was instantly wide awake. And it wasn't the ocean calling her. It was Zoe.

"Rise and shine, sleepyhead!" she said. "It's time to get you in shape for the pageant."

Zoe leaned to one side, and Penny could see someone standing behind her. It was Jack LaLobster, personal trainer extraordinaire. "Hello, Penny," Jack said. "Do you remember me?"

Penny did. He had tried to train her once before, with not-so-great results. "Yes, I remember you, Jack," she said. "Zoe, why—"

"No time to talk," Zoe said. "Exercise first; chat later!"

"What about breakfast?" Penny asked.

"You eat after the workout," LaLobster

told her. "It's your reward for a job well done. Now give me fifty sit-ups."

Penny groaned. What a way to wake up! Next LaLobster made her jog in place, then do press-ups and squats. When LaLobster finally said the workout was over, Zoe brought Penny a plate with one bamboo shoot on it.

"You call this a reward?" Penny complained. LaLobster gently poked Penny in the stomach. "When I see more muscle tone *here*," he said, "you'll see more *here*," pointing to the plate.

Clearly LaLobster didn't remember much from their first meeting. "Mr LaLobster, I am in perfect shape for a panda. I'm supposed to be soft and cuddly, not … hard and … lobster-y."

"Penny, you are indeed in perfect shape for a panda," Zoe said earnestly.

"But we have to make sure you're in *even better* shape."

"It's hard to win a pageant," LaLobster agreed. "But I've worked with many pageant pets in the past. And they always win! You want to be a winner, don't you?"

"Of course she does!" Zoe cheered. "Come on, Penny, ten more sit-ups!"

Penny got down on the floor and groaned again. *This pageant prep isn't easy,* she thought to herself.

Chapter 4
The Perfect Outfit

The pets were starting to plan for the talent part of the contest. Sunil was busy brushing up on his magic tricks. "Welcome to the magic of the Amazing Sunil!" he said. "I would like a volunteer to help me. Yes, you, Mr Green Gecko!"

Vinnie walked over to Sunil with a big

grin on his face.

"Please tell me your name, sir," Sunil said.

"Oh, knock it off, Sunil," Vinnie said.

"Just play along!" Sunil said in a loud stage whisper.

"Oh, OK. I'm Vinnie."

"Nice to meet you, Vinnie! Now pick a card, any card!"

Vinnie picked a card. It was the queen of hearts.

"OK. Please put your card back in the deck," Sunil said. "Now I will read your mind and tell you your card," he went on. "Was it the ace of spades?"

"No."

"The two of clubs?"

"No."

"Hmmm …" Sunil said. "Then maybe it's this card … behind your ear!" He

pulled a card out from behind Vinnie's
ear with a flourish. It was the queen of
hearts.

"Hey, that's pretty good," Vinnie said.

Zoe was busy coaching Penny. "You are
a fabulous ribbon dancer, so that has to
be your talent. Now, what kind of outfit
do you want? Feathers? Sequins? Maybe
something that lights up in the dark!"

Penny was dismayed.
"I don't want to wear
anything like that," she
said. "I want something
easy and fun that I can
move around in. It
should be pretty, but it
should also be simple."

Zoe sighed. "That may work for every
day, but not for a pageant," she said.

Blythe had been listening. "Penny, I promise you, I will make you an outfit that is outstanding and yet simple and chic at the same time. Nothing over-the-top."

"It has to be *a little* over-the-top," Zoe said.

"It will be fashionable but also comfortable, simple and chic," Blythe said firmly. "I always design with my client in mind."

"And that's why you're the best designer ever!" Penny squealed, and gave Blythe a big hug. "This is going to be the best pageant ever!"

Chapter 5
Say Cheese!

All the pets were doing their best to try
to give Penny tips on how to win the
pageant.

"You need to show lots of enthusiasm
and energy!" Minka said, jumping
around.

"You need to smile more," Russell told

her. "You have a great smile. Sparkle! Smile with your eyes!"

"Smile with my eyes?" Penny said doubtfully.

"Think of something that makes you really happy," Blythe said. "That will make your face light up."

Penny's stomach growled. "A big bowl of bamboo shoots would make me really happy!" Penny gave a wide, beautiful smile. She loved that her friends were trying to be helpful, and she told them she'd try to remember all the tips.

Suddenly, Pepper burst into the pet shop. "Paparazzi have been following me all morning," she explained. "They thought I was Kitty Velvet!"

"I find that hard to believe," Zoe said.

"Well, they thought I was Kitty without make-up," Pepper explained. "And," she added indignantly, "some of them told me I looked a lot better!"

The next day, a dashing orange tomcat arrived at the pet shop and shocked everyone by rushing to Pepper's side. "*Mi amore!* My love!" he said. "My name is Benny. When I saw you rushing away from the paparazzi yesterday, I fell in love. I knew there wasn't another cat in the world for me."

"I think there's been a misunderstanding," Pepper told him. "I'm not a cat … I'm a skunk."

Benny laughed heartily. "Beautiful *and* funny!" he said.

Pepper sniffed the air. "What's that smell?" she asked. Then she laughed. "That's funny – that's what people usually ask me!"

"Ah! I brought you a little gift," Benny said, and gave Pepper a toy filled with catnip. Pepper wrinkled her nose at the present. Benny kept lavishing compliments on Pepper. "Your hair ... as dark as midnight ... that beautiful white stripe down your back ... those eyes that haunt my dreams!" But instead of being charmed, Pepper just kept getting more and more annoyed, and she asked Benny to leave.

Penny was surprised by Pepper's attitude. "A lot of creatures have issues with you because of your ... aromas," Penny told her. "Here's someone who really likes you, and you're being so mean to him. And you can never have too many friends!"

Pepper realised Penny was right, and she'd probably been too harsh. "If he comes back, I'll be nice," she promised Penny.

Pepper looked out of the window and realised that she rather liked the tomcat and his compliments. Would he ever come back?

Chapter 6

Big Eyes and Big Lips

"Looking good, Penny! Just five more and you can take a break," Jack LaLobster said.

Penny couldn't believe it. Was Jack actually complimenting her? She took a deep breath and did the press-ups.

Suddenly, Zoe was by LaLobster's side. "Can I show her now, Jack? Pleeeease?"

"Oh, OK," Jack said. "Penny, get ready to be *dazzled*!"

Zoe pranced away and returned with a big box. "For me?" Penny said excitedly. Inside was a long red sequinned feather boa, red satin gloves and a make-up kit.

"For you to wear in the pageant," Zoe told her. "And I told Blythe to match the red to the outfit she's making for you. I'll help you do your make-up of course. I'm thinking big eyes and big lips!"

"Um, I'm thinking *no*," Penny told her. "Thank you very much, but this is so not me."

"Penny, I read today that Kitty Velvet is getting her outfits for the pageant designed in Paris! I just want you to be able to compete." She wrapped the feather boa around Penny's neck and handed her some ribbons.

Penny started twirling the ribbons, but the feathers in the boa made her want to sneeze, the satin gloves made her arms itchy, and it was hard to concentrate on anything when she was starving!

"You can do it, Penny," Zoe said encouragingly. "I know it takes a little getting used to."

"You do look very glamorous, Penny," Pepper said.

Penny decided to give it a try. "OK, I'll be a glamour girl for the pageant. But the minute it's over, Zoe …"

"Yes!" Zoe said, clapping her paws. "That's all I ask, Penny!"

Chapter 7
Look at Me!

The next day, Blythe presented all the pets with their outfits. For Russell, an emerald-green pair of trousers and jacket with slits in the back for his quills to show through. For Sunil, a grey silk suit with a jaunty bow tie. Pepper loved her lacy black dress with a big velvet bow

for her fur. Minka loved her sky-blue sundress so much, it was hard to get her to take it off. Vinnie had a purple tuxedo! And even though Zoe wasn't in the competition, Blythe made her a fabulous hot  pink gown with grey satin along the hem and collar. But the crowning glory was a beach hat festooned with ribbons and sparkles and lace, and little round balls filled with glittery seashells. Blythe saved Penny's outfit for last. It was a simple red silk shorts and tank top combo, but she also had a beach hat – a beautiful ruby-red straw hat with a thick red satin ribbon around the crown. Penny adored her outfit – it was both beautiful and simple at the same time.

And she promised the pets she'd wear the gloves and feather boa for the talent competition.

"Let's go outside," Blythe said to Penny. "I want to see how the outfit looks while you move around."

They all went outside and watched as Penny practised her ribbon-dancing routine. It started off OK, but as Penny started thinking about the pageant and imagining all eyes on her, suddenly she started fumbling around and getting her ribbons all tangled up in a ball.

The pets all tried to offer advice.

"They say if you're nervous about a performance, you should look for a friendly face in the crowd and concentrate on that person," Minka said. "Look for me, Penny!"

"Why should she look for you?" Zoe

says. "She should look for me!"

It didn't take long for all the pets to start arguing about who was the best pet for Penny to focus on. They were so busy chattering, they didn't even hear the clicking of a camera lens or the rustling of a person in the bushes.

"Hello, Priscilla? Claude here. I just found the most fabulous outfit for Kitty. It's perfect – a beautiful shade of deep ruby red. We need to call Kitty's designer and send him this photo, pronto. The pageant is just a few days away!"

Chapter 8
Talent Show

The next couple of days were quiet, as all the pets were working on their talents. Minka decided she would create a painting, live in front of the judges. "It will be exciting – inspired!" she said.

Russell decided he would sing. "I will croon a love song," he said. "Perhaps

some hedgehog will hear me and fall in love."

Although Pepper enjoyed doing stand-up comedy, she decided to perform a classical piano piece. Pepper played well, but the pets felt it was slow and dreary.

"Can't you pep it up a little?" Vinnie asked. "Play something snappy, something people will dance to!"

But Pepper refused to change her selection. "I'm sure the judges will love it," she said. "What are you going to do, Vinnie?"

"I'm so glad you asked," Vinnie said. "Music, please, Sunil."

Sunil touched his phone and the song *Singin' in the Rain* started playing. Vinnie whipped out a tiny umbrella and

started dancing. Even Pepper had to admit it was pretty cute.

Meanwhile, Penny's ribbon dancing was coming along beautifully. When she rehearsed for a second time in front of the pets, she made sure to focus on one pet as she twirled. Once she focused on Zoe, another time on Pepper, and so on.

With her friends cheering her on, she started to think being in a pageant wasn't so bad. "Meet this year's perfect pet winner – Penny," she said to herself. It had a nice ring to it!

Chapter 9
Costume Calamity

The first thing all the pets saw the next morning was Benny the tomcat at the front door again. Blythe let him in. He saw (and heard) Pepper playing the keyboard.

"My love, you never cease to amaze me," he said adoringly. "Funny, smart, beautiful and talented!"

Pepper gave Benny an annoyed look and was about to say something when Penny caught her eye and Pepper remembered that she shouldn't be mean.

"Benny, I don't know how more clearly to say this – I'm not a cat, I'm a skunk. The only thing I can think of to prove it to you is to spray you, and you do not want that!"

"My love, you could not smell more wonderful to me if you were standing in a garden of roses," Benny said. "You are so lovely – much lovelier than that Kitty Velvet. in her red feather boa and straw hat."

At these words, Pepper looked

up with a start. "What did you just say? About Kitty Velvet's outfit?"

"I was saying that you look better than she does … look!" Benny held up a phone and showed Pepper a photo of Kitty Velvet … and she was wearing a nearly exact replica of Penny's outfit!

"This is a disaster!" Pepper exclaimed.

"I agree the hat is a bit much, but the rest of the outfit is quite nice," Benny said.

"Not the outfit! I mean … never mind, it will take too long to explain. I'm really sorry, but I can't chat with you now. Can you come back another time?"

"For you, my love, I will wait for ever," Benny said as he left the pet shop.

Pepper rushed over to Blythe. "Go online and do a search for 'Kitty Velvet pageant outfit'."

Blythe opened up her laptop and searched. She gasped. "Someone must have taken a picture of Penny when she was rehearsing in her outfit, and sent it to Kitty!"

"But can't we sue them for stealing her outfit?"

"Not really," Blythe said. "They were very sneaky! They changed enough so it's not an exact copy. And they posted a photo right away so if anything people will think *Penny* copied *Kitty*!"

"But you're the greatest designer in the world," Zoe said. "I'm sure you can make something even more wonderful."

"I'll try," Blythe said. "But I used up all the fabric I bought."

Penny was devastated. "Maybe it's not meant to be," she said sadly. "Maybe I shouldn't enter the contest."

"Don't say that, Penny!" Blythe said. "I'll figure something out."

In the meantime, the pets had huddled into a group and were deep in discussion.

Russell turned to Blythe, acting as the spokesperson. "Blythe, we would all like you to take pieces of our outfits to make a new one for Penny," he said.

"Well, I think you are the sweetest pets in the world," Blythe said. "But I'm still not sure I'll have enough material to make a whole new outfit."

Just as Blythe and all the pets were considering this, Benny returned.

"Hello, my love!" he said cheerfully. "I couldn't stay away any longer. Do you have time now to chat?"

Pepper sighed. "Hello, Benny," she said. "I really can't talk now. I'm in the middle of a crisis."

"What kind of crisis?" Benny asked. "Perhaps I can help."

"That's very sweet of you," Pepper said. "But I don't think you can. We need fabric for costumes for the Perfect Pet Pageant. So unless you know somebody who works in a fabric store—"

"*Mi amore!*" Benny cried. "My owner is a seamstress. She always has tons of fabric."

Blythe had been listening. "Benny, that sounds great," she said. "But what excuse do I give for showing up at your doorstep?"

Benny leaped into Blythe's arms. "Take me home. Tell her you found me, crying and

hungry. She's always worried about me. I do run away a lot," he admitted.

"Well, it's worth a shot," Blythe said.

Benny looked back at Pepper contentedly. "I am going to be a hero for you, my love!"

Penny looked at Pepper and smiled. "What did I tell you, Pepper? You can never have enough friends!"

Chapter 10
Fabulous Fabric

Fortunately, Benny didn't live far from the pet shop. A sweet, grey-haired old lady answered the door. "Yes?" she asked, then looked down. "Benny!" the woman cried. "I've been so worried about you!"

"He's fine," Blythe said. "I found him wandering in front of the pet shop where

I work, noticed his tags, and brought him here."

"Oh, I can't thank you enough!" the woman said. "Come in, dear! I'm Sarah."

Blythe followed. "I'm Blythe," she said.

Blythe immediately noticed a huge sewing machine in the front room. "What a beautiful sewing machine," she said. "Do you sew a lot?"

"Why, yes, I make all my own clothes," Sarah said proudly.

"I love to sew, too," Blythe told her. "As a matter of fact, I'm in the middle of a sewing project, and I'm in a bit of a dilemma. I ran out of fabric and—"

Before Blythe could finish, Sarah took her by the hand. "Oh, please follow me!" She took Blythe into a small room filled with mannequins and boxes of fabric, buttons, lace and ribbons. "If there's anything here that can help you, please help yourself!"

Benny purred contentedly in Sarah's arms, then turned to look at Blythe and gave her a big wink!

Blythe looked through the boxes and found the perfect fabric – it was a deep sapphire-blue satin. Then she had another idea – she'd trim the outfit using pieces from the other pets' costumes, so it would be like they all had a part in creating Penny's look.

Blythe told Sarah about the Perfect Pet Pageant. "It sounds wonderful!" Sarah exclaimed. "I think I'll enter Benny!" she cried. "Won't that be fun, Benny-kins?"

Benny looked at Blythe, alarmed, and let out a yowl.

"Oooh, I think he's excited!" Sarah exclaimed.

All Blythe could do was laugh. "Excited isn't the word!"

Chapter 11
Furry
Fall-Out

"No, no, Penny! Pay attention!" Zoe
was trying to give Penny some tips, and
things weren't going very well. "Now
watch," Zoe said. "Pretend I'm walking
down a runway." Zoe walked slowly,
turning her head first left, then right.
She batted her lashes, smiled, tossed her

head back and laughed.

"What are you laughing at?" Penny asked.

"Nothing," Zoe said. "I'm just laughing so the photographers can take a picture of me that shows off all my beautiful white teeth."

"Ohhh," Penny said.

"OK," Zoe said. "Now you try."

"All right," Penny agreed. She took a deep breath and began walking slowly. She tried batting her eyelashes, but she just looked like she was blinking really hard. She forced out a hearty laugh. "Ha-ha-ha!" Penny said.

Zoe looked at her, annoyed. "What was that?" she asked.

"Well, it's hard for me

to fake laughing," Penny said.

Minka had been watching. "You know, Zoe, what works for you may not necessarily work for Penny," she said. "You really shouldn't force her to do anything."

"You don't understand," Zoe replied. "I'm her mentor. Penny knows anything I tell her to do is for her own good. Isn't that right, Penny?"

"Well…" Penny hesitated.

"Well what? Why are you hesitating?" Zoe demanded.

"Minka has a point," Penny said. "You are being … bossy."

"There!" Minka said triumphantly. "I knew it!"

"You knew what? How to cause trouble?

Look, Minka, things were going just fine until you butted in."

"I don't think so, Zoe," Minka said. "I think Penny has probably been unhappy for a while. She's just too nice to say anything."

Zoe whirled around to look at Penny. "Is this true?" she demanded. "You simply cannot be my protégée if this is how you feel. And you either agree with me and trust that I'm teaching you with the best intentions, or you agree with Minka. And if you agree with Minka, we can't be friends. You have to choose!"

Penny felt tears well up in her eyes. "Don't make me choose … I can't. You're both my friends!"

"Then I'll make it easy for you," Zoe replied. "I am no longer your mentor!" With that, Zoe flounced off.

"Nooo …" Penny wailed. Now what was she going to do?

Later that day, Sunil and Vinnie were discussing the situation.

"Well, I can see Zoe's side," Sunil said. "Penny did agree to have Zoe as her mentor."

"But I can see Minka's side," Vinnie told him. "Zoe can be really bossy, and a lot of what she wants Penny to do is not her style at all."

"That's the point," Sunil said. "Zoe is training Penny to compete in a pageant. She's not supposed to be herself."

"Why are you always so stubborn?" Vinnie said. "Can't you even consider my point of view?"

"Can't you even

consider mine?" Sunil cried.

"Don't talk to me!"

"Fine! Don't talk to me, either!"

Pepper bounced into the room. "Hey, what's going on?" she asked.

"Oh, be quiet, Pepper!" Vinnie yelled.

"Yeah, just leave us alone," Sunil said.

Russell had been observing all this quietly. *Uh-oh*, he thought. *I'd better fill Blythe in on what's been going on.*

Chapter 12
Sorrys All Round

"And so that's what's been going on," Russell said. "Basically everyone is mad at each other."

"This is terrible!" Blythe said. "We have to get everyone speaking again."

Blythe had finished everyone's outfits, so she figured maybe if everyone tried

them on, that would get them speaking again.

And it did – only not in the way Blythe hoped!

Zoe tried on her pink gown. She looked and felt beautiful until Minka muttered, "Pink is a very sweet colour. Too bad it doesn't match the personality of the person wearing it."

"I am as sweet as pie," Zoe said indignantly. "Just ask anybody. As for you … well, I get a little seasick looking at all that blue."

"Hey!" Blythe said, upset. "I made that, Zoe!"

"Oh, the craftsmanship is outstanding," Zoe told her. "It's just too bad you don't have a better model to show it off."

Sunil was admiring himself in a full-length mirror when Vinnie walked by and coughed, "Goofball in a goofy bow tie!"

"Whoever heard of a purple tuxedo?" Sunil sneered.

"OK, this has got to stop," Blythe said. "The pageant is coming up very soon, and you have to all make up or…"

"Or what, Blythe?" Zoe asked. "It's obvious we aren't going to be friends any time soon."

To break the tension, Russell turned on the TV. A celebrity reporter was talking about Kitty Velvet. "I met with Kitty Velvet's owner today," the reporter was saying. "And I have to say, she is pretty confident about Kitty winning the Perfect Pet Pageant. 'Kitty is more beautiful and talented than any pets around here,' her owner told me. 'I mean, who is the competition? A goofy dancing gecko? A silly panda waving her silly ribbons?'"

All the pets were silent for a moment.

"We've been so stupid," Pepper said.

"We've forgotten we wanted Penny to win because we love her," Sunil said.

"And here we are fighting and making everything worse," Zoe added.

"And that stupid Kitty Velvet thinks she's going to win!" Vinnie fumed. "Goofy dancing gecko indeed!"

"Well," Sunil said, "first, we apologise to each other. Then we have to find Penny and apologise to her. And third, we make sure Penny has all our support and kicks that Kitty Velvet's butt!" He turned to Vinnie. "I'm sorry, buddy."

"Aw, I'm sorry, too, Sunil."

"Zoe? Minka? Don't you two have something you want to say to each other?" Blythe asked.

There was nothing but silence between the beautiful Cavalier King Charles spaniel and the spider monkey.

Pepper broke the silence.

"Oh for goodness' sake. Zoe, Minka, both of you! Say you're sorry! DO IT FOR PENNY!"

Those words seemed to wake the two pets up. Suddenly, they couldn't say they were sorry fast enough.

"I shouldn't have questioned your mentoring skills," Minka said. "I'm so sorry, Zoe!"

"I can be a bit bossy," Zoe admitted. "I need to learn to be a better listener. I'm sorry, too, Minka!"

"OK, next we need to apologise to Penny," Sunil said.

Penny was in bed, under the covers, sobbing. All the pets sat in a circle on the top of the bed.

Blythe spoke up. "Penny, everyone is here, and they all want to speak with you."

At this, the sniffling grew softer, and then finally, two large grey eyes appeared over the blanket. "What do you want?" Penny asked.

Russell decided to be the spokesperson. "Penny, we're sorry. We all got so wrapped up in how we thought things should go, we forgot about the most important person here – you!"

"Penny, you should act however you

want in the pageant," Zoe said. "And I will support you. I love you!"

"We all love you, Penny," Minka said. "Can you ever forgive us?"

"Well …" Penny hesitated. "Of course I can! You guys are my best friends. I forgive you!"

"Fantastic," Vinnie cheered. "Now it's time to kick some pageant butt!"

Chapter 13
The Perfect Accessory

The Perfect Pet Pageant was getting a lot of publicity because of Kitty Velvet. One night Blythe was watching the news, and she saw Sarah, Benny's owner, being interviewed.

"Pepper, look, it's Sarah!" Blythe said.

Sarah was holding Benny and petting

him. Benny didn't look very pleased.

"Excuse me, ma'am, but I was wondering if you're entering your cat in the Perfect Pet Pageant?" the reporter asked.

"Oh, yes! I'm looking forward to it, and so is Benny," Sarah said.

"And what will Benny perform?" the reporter asked. "What is Benny good at?"

"Oh, I haven't decided," Sarah said. "Running away from home? He's very good at that!"

At this point, Benny looked right into the camera and meowed loudly. Sarah and the reporter just laughed. But in the Littlest Pet Shop, Blythe and all the pets heard, "Pepper, my love, I miss youuuuuu!" All the pets cracked up.

The pets decided it was time to brush up on their talents. Minka had been

practising her on-the-spot paintings. So
far she'd painted a banana tree, a bowl
of bananas and a pile of bananas.

"Shouldn't you paint something a little
more exciting than bananas?" Sunil
asked.

Minka shrugged.
"I'm a monkey.
People will expect
me to paint
bananas," she said.

Vinnie was
practising his
Singin' in the Rain number. "Blythe, this
would be so much better if I had tap
shoes," he said.

"Vinnie, there are no such thing as
gecko-sized shoes, much less tap shoes,"
Blythe told him.

Russell was singing his love song. He

closed his eyes and sang passionately. When he opened his eyes again, he saw all the pets had their hands covering their ears. "Oh dear," he said. "I guess I'm not as wonderful a singer as I thought." He looked over at Blythe for help.

"Maybe another type of romantic performance?" Blythe suggested. "Maybe recite a romantic poem instead?"

"That's a great idea!" Russell said. "An original poem – one I that I will write myself! What rhymes with love? Love ... dove ... glove ... blue sky above ..." He hurried off in search of a pencil and paper.

Pepper sat down at the piano to play her classical piece. But after the first few notes, she stopped. "Playing this song makes me think of Benny," she said. "I miss him!"

The only pet who didn't seem to need any practice was Penny.

"Penny, when you twirl those ribbons, you are poetry in motion," Sunil said admiringly.

"Thank you," Penny said. She was getting more and more excited about the pageant as the days went on.

Blythe walked over to Penny, holding a box. "I've finished your outfit for the pageant, Penny," she said. "And I have a little surprise for you." Instead of a feather boa, Blythe had made Penny a multicoloured scarf with pieces of fabric from all the other pets' costumes.

"So when you're performing, remember you're going to be carrying a little piece of all your friends with you,"

Blythe said. "So there's no reason to be nervous or scared. All the while you are onstage, you will be covered in your friends' love."

"Wow, that's just beautiful, Blythe," Zoe said.

"It's beautiful because it's true," Minka said.

"Let the games begin!" Penny said. "I'm ready!"

Chapter 14
Showtime

The big day was finally here! The boardwalk was packed with people, pets, reporters and photographers. Blythe spotted the Biskit twins, who somehow managed to look excited and bored at the same time.

"Hello, Blythe. Is she here?" Whittany Biskit asked.

"Is who here?" Blythe said.

"Oh, come on," Brittany said. "Kitty Velvet. She's the only reason anyone who's anyone is here!"

"I don't know about that," Blythe said. "I'm pretty excited about entering my pets."

"Of course you are," Whittany said. "We know one of your little dogs won last year, but that was before there was any real competition."

Zoe heard this and started growling.

"Come on, Whittany," Brittany said. "This is boring. Pets bore me."

"Your father owns a pet shop!" Blythe said, confused.

"Whatever," Whittany said. "See you

later, Blythe."

Benny the tomcat had escaped from his owner, again, to see Pepper.

"My love, you are here!" he said happily.

"Hello, Benny," Pepper said with a laugh. "Don't you look nice!"

Benny was decked out in a black tuxedo. He sighed. "Sarah made me wear this," he said. "It's just one more thing I will endure to see you!"

"Benny!" Sarah was suddenly between them. Sarah looked at Blythe. "Hello, dear," she said as she scooped Benny up. "I said his biggest talent is running away. Well, good luck to you and all your lovely pets!"

"And good luck to you and Benny," Blythe said.

Suddenly, there was a flurry of cameras

clicking. "There she is!" someone yelled

A stretch limo had pulled up. A chauffeur opened a door, and out stepped a very fashionable young woman walking a cat on a leash. The cat was Kitty Velvet, and she was wearing the ruby-red outfit Blythe had originally designed for Penny. Kitty Velvet walked slowly and turned every time she heard a camera click. She smiled and purred and batted impossibly long lashes.

"Fake eyelashes," Zoe muttered under her breath.

"Don't worry, Penny," Minka told her. "Your new outfit is even better than the one Kitty stole from us. And you're real and she's just a big fake!"

"Thank you, Minka," Penny said.
Truth be told, Penny was a little nervous.
Kitty Velvet seemed so cool, calm and
collected. Would she be able to hold her
own against her?

The master of ceremonies walked up
to a microphone to start the pageant.
"Greetings, everyone, and thank you for
coming out for our fifth annual Perfect
Pet Pageant. I'm Gerry Geralds, and
we're going to have a great time today,
aren't we?" Everyone cheered. "All right,
then! We will first have our contestants
walk down the runway with their owners.
Pets, it's your turn to shine!"

Some of the pets raced down the
runway. One puppy even peed on it! One
angry cat hissed at everyone the entire
way down. Minka loved it – she bounced
down the runway, waving at the crowd.

"Isn't she cute?" kids whispered to each other, and snapped photos with their phones. Sunil was a little shy and kept his eyes down. Pepper was nervous and started to let out a bit of an aroma, but was able to keep it under control. Russell stayed close to Blythe, and Vinnie was a natural ham.

But the real surprise was Penny! She strutted down the runway as if it was the most natural thing in the world. She looked out into the audience and saw Jack LaLobster nodding at her. She thought of a big plate of bamboo shoots and gave everyone a beautiful smile.

"Oooh, that panda is so adorable," one little girl sighed. Everyone was in love with Penny!

Next up was Benny. He kept pawing at the bow tie, which everyone thought was hilarious. "The things I do for love," Benny muttered to himself. Then he caught Pepper's eye and gave her a big wink!

Just then, a murmur went through the crowd. Kitty Velvet was gliding down the runway, purring loudly. Her glossy black fur with that unique white stripe, her huge green eyes – *you* couldn't help staring at the magnificent cat.

"She's so cool," Whittany whispered to her twin, Brittany.

"Totally," Brittany agreed.

After all the pets had taken their walk, Gerry Geralds walked to the microphone again. "Now that we've seen all the pets, the next step will be to talk to their owners and find out a little more about them all." The crowd applauded. "All right, then!" He consulted a list. "Our first pet up will be … Russell Ferguson with Blythe Baxter."

"We're on!" Blythe whispered to Russell.

"Hello, Blythe! My, this is a fine-looking porcupine," Gerry said.

"Grrr …" Russell growled quietly.

Blythe smiled politely. "Russell is not a porcupine, Gerry. He's a hedgehog."

"A hedgehog! What's the difference?" Gerry asked.

"Grrr …" Russell growled again, this time a bit louder.

"Well, a hedgehog's quills are not barbed, and they're not poisonous," Blythe said. "And the quills are mostly hollow, which makes them light, but strong!"

"Fascinating!" Gerry said. "And why would you say Russell the hedgehog is the perfect pet, Blythe?"

"Russell is very loyal," Blythe said. "He's very devoted to me, and keeps me company in the pet shop where I work. He's very sweet and smart, and hedgehogs eat pesky insects, which is a very good thing!"

"Indeed it is!" Gerry said cheerfully. "OK, let's hear it for Russell the hedgehog!" The audience applauded politely.

"Next up we have Sarah Shaw and her cat Benny," Gerry said.

Sarah and Benny walked over to Gerry. Benny was scowling and tugging crossly at his collar.

"Awww, someone looks like he doesn't want to be here," Gerry said.

"Oh, but I'm so glad he's here!" Sarah said. "Benny is my best friend. He brings so much happiness to my life."

"Well, that certainly sounds like a potential perfect pet. Let's hear it for Benny!" Once again the audience applauded.

"OK, next up we have Blythe and Sunil! Hello again, Blythe!"

"Hello. I'll be up here a lot because I work in a pet shop," Blythe explained.

"And tell me about your little weasel there, Sunil."

"Weasel?" Sunil said, insulted. But except for Blythe, the other people watching just heard an indignant squeal. Everyone laughed!

 78

"Sunil isn't a weasel," Blythe said patiently. "He is a mongoose. And he's wonderful. He may seem quiet and shy, but did you know a mongoose can kill a snake?"

"No, I didn't know that! Seems like a good little guy to have around. Thank you, Blythe and Sunil! Next up we have Vinnie and Mrs Twombly."

Mrs Twombly walked over to Gerry, holding Vinnie. "Tell me about your little lizard friend, Mrs Twombly," Gerry said.

"Well, this here is Vinnie," Mrs Twombly said. "He is a gecko. He's not quite as cuddly as some other types of pets, but he's a wonderful dancer, as you shall see!"

"I can't wait!" Gerry said. "Thank you, Mrs Twombly. Who do we have next? Why, it's our friend Blythe again … with Pepper … the … now this time I hope I'm wrong! Is Pepper a skunk?"

"Indeed she is, Gerry," Blythe said.

"Don't listen to them, my love!" Benny yelled. But all anyone heard was a cat yowling.

"Is it … *safe* to have Pepper here, Blythe?" Gerry asked.

"Of course," Blythe said. "She doesn't spray unless she's upset or angry."

"And you're not going to make me angry, are you?" Pepper asked, looking up at Gerry with an evil gleam in her eye.

"Hmm … I don't like the way she's looking at me," Gerry said. "Let's move on."

A few other pets and their owners were

introduced. Minka kept fidgeting.

"Minka, calm down," Blythe said. "You're making me nervous!"

When Gerry announced Minka's and Blythe's names, Minka bounded right over to Gerry.

"Well, hello, Minka!" Gerry said.

"Minka is very bubbly and friendly," Blythe said. "That's one of the reasons she's the perfect pet!"

"She certainly is adorable," Gerry agreed. Suddenly, Minka leaped on to his head!

"Hey!" Gerry shouted.

Blythe giggled. "I'm sorry, Gerry," she said. "I guess she thinks you're a tree!" Everyone laughed

as Blythe said, "Come down now, Minka," and Minka jumped into her arms.

"Now, next up we have a cat. This cat needs no introduction. So why am I introducing her? Ha-ha-ha. Everyone, meet Kitty Velvet and her owner, Priscilla Lee."

"About time," Whittany Biskit muttered, and got her phone ready.

"I must say, Kitty, red is your colour," Gerry said. Blythe just shook her head. She still couldn't believe someone had stolen her designs and given them to Kitty! "And, Priscilla, why would you say Kitty is the perfect pet?"

"Well, just look at her!" Priscilla said. "Isn't she gorgeous? Who wouldn't want a little Kitty Velvet in their life?" The crowd applauded and cheered.

"Everyone seems to agree!" Gerry

chirped. "Now we have one last contestant. Blythe, please come back and bring Penny!"

Blythe and Penny walked over. Penny was absolutely glowing in her sapphire-blue outfit. Everyone was oohing and aahing over the adorable panda.

"Wow, Blythe!" Gerry said. "What a cutie Penny is!"

"Yes, she is," Blythe agreed. "Penny is cuddly and loving, and has the biggest heart of all the animals in my pet shop. She brings joy and happiness wherever she goes. Penny is simply the best!"

At this point, Penny turned to the audience and waved. Everyone started snapping photos! Then Penny turned to Gerry and gave him a huge hug. The audience went crazy!

Gerry smiled and said, "Well ... I don't

know what to say except … watch out, Kitty Velvet!"

In the audience, Priscilla Lee took out her phone and made a call. "You didn't tell me about the panda!" she hissed, and hung up.

"Woo-hoo! Go Penny!" Zoe cheered.

Chapter 15
On with the Show

Next was the talent part of the pageant. There were the usual dogs and puppies rolling over, playing dead and fetching various objects, parakeets that said funny things their owners had taught them, and an occasional pet that got stage fright and just ran away.

Blythe gathered her little group together for a pep talk. "OK, how's everybody feeling?" she asked.

"I feel great!" Russell said.

"Never better," Vinnie replied.

"I'm a bit nervous, but I'll be all right," Sunil said.

"I'm good," Pepper said.

"I can't wait to go on!" Minka said, jumping around impatiently. "Am I next?"

At that moment, Zoe and Jack LaLobster appeared. "You're all doing great!" Zoe said. "I'm so proud of you."

"And the word on the street is the pageant is going to come down to Penny and Kitty Velvet," Jack LaLobster said.

"How are you feeling, Penny?"

"I'm …. OK," Penny said.

Blythe was handing Penny the scarf made from all the pets' costumes, and her big brimmed hat, which she'd promised to wear.

"Do I really need to wear all this?" she asked.

"Yes!" Zoe said emphatically.

Blythe led Penny over to a full-length mirror. "See? You look amazing!"

"I guess," Penny agreed. "It's just so not me. It's more like … her." She happened to glance to her right and see Kitty Velvet being fussed over by two or three different pet handlers.

"You are Penny, and she is Kitty," Blythe

said. "You each have your own style. Don't worry about her. You're going to be great!"

"Thanks, Blythe," Penny said. "I'm ready, I guess!"

"Fantastic," Blythe said. "On with the show!"

Chapter 16
Class Acts

Sarah was worried about Benny. She'd tried to make him do various cute things for his talent (chase after a fake mouse, sit at a toy piano and pretend to play), but he would have nothing to do with it.

When Benny's name was announced, Gerry Geralds asked Sarah what Benny

was going to do. "I think he's going to …
sing?" Sarah said.

"Wonderful!" Gerry said. "Benny, the
stage is yours."

Benny walked over to centre stage and
started meowing. A lot. The people in
the audience sniggered. But Blythe and
the pets heard this:

> "Pepper, you are the spice of my
> life.
>
> Pepper, you make
> everything nice!
>
> Pepper, how can I
> make you see that you're
> the only one for me?
>
> With your hair so dark and
> your eyes so bright,
> You're who I dream of every night!
> Pepper, Pepper!
> How can I make you see

You're the only one for me?"

Pepper covered her face with her paws in embarrassment.

"That was a lovely …er … song, Benny," Gerry said. "But you know, I couldn't help noticing Benny kept looking over at Pepper during his song! Maybe he has a crush on the skunk!"

"She … is … not … a skunk!" Benny hissed at Gerry. But of course he just saw (and heard) a cat hissing at him, and so he quickly backed off.

"Well. Why don't we have Pepper Clark perform next?" Gerry asked. Blythe and Pepper walked to centre stage. Blythe gently put down a small keyboard in front of Pepper.

"Pepper plays the piano?" Gerry asked, shocked.

"Indeed she does," Blythe said.

"All right, then," Gerry said.

Pepper took a deep breath and began playing her classical piece. To all the pets (and Benny and Blythe), it sounded wonderful, but to the audience, it was simply an animal hitting keys with its paws. Still, they were entertained and applauded politely.

She's the most wonderful cat in the world, Benny thought with a blissful sigh.

"Next up, we have Sunil Nevla," Gerry announced. Sunil took the stage a bit timidly, and Blythe handed him a small deck of cards.

"Sunil is actually a wonderful magician," Blythe said. "Everyone, meet the amazing Sunil!"

Sunil bowed slightly and received thunderous applause!

"The amazing Sunil needs a volunteer,"

Blythe continued. "Gerry, would you do the honours?"

"Me?" Gerry exclaimed. "Why, I'd be delighted."

Sunil scattered the cards in front of him and looked up at Blythe expectantly.

"He would like you to pick a card," Blythe said.

Gerry picked a card and showed it to the audience. It was the ten of clubs.

Sunil looked down at the deck. Blythe told Gerry to put his card back in the deck.

Sunil tried to shuffle the cards but ended up simply scattering them madly about the stage. He grabbed a card in his mouth and showed it to Gerry. It was *not* the ten of clubs. Gerry shook his head. Sunil grabbed another, and Gerry smiled and shook his head again. Sunil whispered to Blythe to look behind Gerry's ear, but there was no card there.

"I don't understand. It worked perfectly with Vinnie!" Sunil said. Of course the audience only heard a mongoose chattering, but they were still charmed by Sunil's outfit and the fact that he'd tried to perform a magic trick. He got a huge round of applause.

"Next up is Minka Mark," Gerry said. He smiled as he saw Blythe return with Minka perched on her shoulder. Blythe was also carrying a small paintbrush, white paper and a can of yellow paint.

"Aaah, do we have an artist in our midst?" Gerry asked.

"We do!" Blythe said. "Minka would

 94

love to paint for you."

Blythe sat Minka down and Minka immediately got to work, painting yellow crescents.

"What are those … yellow moons?" Gerry said. "Oh, wait! I get it! Bananas, of course!"

Everyone applauded, and someone in the audience actually yelled out, "How much for the painting?"

"I'm sorry, Minka's artwork is not for sale," Blythe replied.

Vinnie was next! Blythe brought Vinnie to the stage and handed him his little paper umbrella. She played the song *Singin' in the Rain* on her phone as

Vinnie pranced around. Everyone loved the dancing gecko!

Now it was Russell's turn. "Russell is going to recite a love poem," Blythe told the audience. "And perhaps there is a lovely hedgehog in the audience somewhere that will hear him," she said to Gerry.

"Or maybe a porcupine?" Gerry suggested with a wink.

"I … am … not … a porcupine," Russell muttered.

Russell cleared his throat and began. Of course the audience heard nothing but a hedgehog squealing. But Russell's poem was so sincere it brought Blythe and the other pets close to tears.

"Aww, it almost sounded as though he was really trying to say something, didn't it, folks?" Gerry said to the crowd. "Next up will be the lovely Kitty Velvet!"

Kitty Velvet walked to centre stage with her owner, Priscilla Lee.

"And what will Kitty's talent be today?" Gerry asked.

"Kitty will be showcasing some of the expressions she uses in her modelling," Priscilla said.

"Well, that certainly sounds interesting and different," Gerry said. "The stage is all yours, Kitty and Priscilla!"

"Thank you," Priscilla said. She turned to Kitty. "Kitty, show us *sweet*!" she said.

Kitty gave a heart-melting look and rested her face on her two front paws.

"Awwww …" the audience murmured.

"Next, Kitty, show us *sad*," Priscilla said.

Kitty responded with big misty eyes about to brim over with tears.

"OMG, I feel like I could cry myself right now," Brittany Biskit whispered to Whittany.

"Now show us *angry*!" Priscilla said. Kitty hissed at the audience and made a scratching gesture with her paw.

"And finally, show us *love*, Kitty!"

Kitty put a paw to her face and appeared to be blowing the audience a kiss. The audience ate it up and burst into thunderous applause.

"Wow, she's really good," Zoe said to Jack LaLobster. Would Penny be able to compete?

Chapter 17
And the Winner Is ...

"And our final contestant is Penny,"
Gerry said. All the pets huddled together
to watch as Blythe brought Penny out.
"What is Penny's talent, Blythe?" Gerry
asked.

"Penny is a ribbon twirler," Blythe said.

"A ribbon twirler!" Gerry repeated.

"I can't wait to see that!"

Blythe handed Penny her ribbons, whispered "Good luck!" and stepped back.

Penny began her routine, slowly at first. But right away, Zoe could tell there was a problem.

"Something's wrong," Zoe whispered to LaLobster. "She's not … sparkling at all!"

Zoe was right. Penny wasn't sparkling. It was the fancy scarf. It was the huge hat. It was the silk gloves. It was the make-up on her eyes. She was so uncomfortable and unhappy! She suddenly dropped the ribbons and burst into tears.

"Oh noooo!" Zoe moaned.

Blythe was on stage in a flash. She immediately cuddled Penny.

Meanwhile, Priscilla Lee looked down at Kitty Velvet in her arms. "I think a certain kitty is going home with a tiara tonight!" she whispered happily. Kitty purred in agreement.

Gerry Geralds was uncertain what to do. "Blythe, does Penny want to forfeit the talent part?" he asked.

"No, no, please!" Blythe begged. "Just give me a minute." She stared at Penny, who had stopped weeping but was now sniffling.

"Penny, you don't have to wear anything you don't want to," Blythe told her. "I'm sorry we tried to make you a glamour girl! You go out there and just be Penny. I promise you, that will be more than special enough!"

Penny began her routine again. First, she took off the long silk gloves. Then the scarf that was both itchy and hot. Finally, she tossed the beach hat aside. As pretty as it was, it was making her feel dizzy. But as she tossed the hat, a couple of shiny balls filled with seashells bounced off the hat. Without even thinking about it, Penny reached out to catch them. They were so pretty, Penny thought, it would be a shame if they broke! The audience applauded. Then Penny put the balls down and began her ribbon-twirling routine.

Freed, Penny was in the zone. She was twirling her beautiful multicoloured ribbons faster and faster.

"It looks like she's creating a rainbow!" Mrs Twombly gasped.

Penny was glowing with happiness! She'd never looked more beautiful.

"Pen-ny Ling! Pen-ny Ling!" the

audience cheered.

As Penny finished her routine, the audience gave her a standing ovation!

It didn't take the judges long to decide the winner.

"Was there ever any doubt?" Gerry Geralds asked the audience. "The winner of this year's Perfect Pet Pageant is Miss Penny!"

"YESSSS!" all the pets cheered as Blythe gave Penny a huge hug.

Blythe whispered in Penny's ear, "I'm so proud of you! I knew you could do it!"

Benny the tomcat found Pepper in the crowd. "My love, I was hoping you would win. But your friend Penny really is a wonderful performer."

"Yes, she is," Pepper replied. But she

was thinking hard. How would she ever get Benny to believe she was not a cat? "Benny, look. You have to believe me when I say …"

Suddenly, a strange look crossed Benny's face. "What is that smell?" he said. And Pepper realised it was her! She was so nervous about talking to Benny, she started to smell … just a little bit.

"My love, is that … you?" Benny asked, slowly walking a bit away from her.

Pepper sighed. "Yes, Benny, it's me."

"So you really are a skunk!" he said in amazement.

"Yes, I really am," Pepper laughed.

"Attention, please!" Gerry Geralds

said. "It's now time to crown our new perfect pet!" He held up a sparkly tiara and placed it on Penny's head. Everyone cheered!

"And now, Miss Penny, we have a special prize, selected especially for you," Gerry said. He handed Penny a large silver platter – piled high with bamboo shoots! "And may I just say, congratu—" But before he could even get the word out, Penny dived face-first into the delicious platter of bamboo and started eating away.

"Woo-hoo! Three cheers for Penny!" Blythe yelled as all the pets laughed and cheered for Penny, natural beauty *and* winner of the Perfect Pet Pageant!

The End

Read on for a sneak peek
at another
Littlest Pet Shop adventure,

Art from
the Heart

Minka the monkey burst into the
Littlest Pet Shop, chattering with
excitement as her owner dropped her
off. She stood in the middle of the store
and shook wildly, sending droplets of
water scattering throughout the room.
And no wonder – it was pouring with
rain outside!

Still chattering, Minka catapulted
through the curtain that separated Day

Camp from the rest of the store and skidded to a sudden stop. Something was wrong – very wrong. Sure, it was dark and stormy outside…but why did her friends' faces look so dark and stormy, too?

Fashion fanatic Zoe the King Charles spaniel was organising her nail polish dejectedly.

Russell the hedgehog, normally a bustling bundle of energy, was staring out of the window, absent-mindedly tallying bolts of lightning.

Penny Ling, the gentle panda, was muttering to herself as she attempted to thread a needle.

Even Pepper the skunk, who could turn just about anything into a joke, looked glum as she sprawled across a pet bed and stared at the ceiling.

Well, this is no good, Minka thought.

Where are Vinnie and Sunil? They'll know how to brighten things up.

Minka found Vinnie the gecko and Sunil the mongoose in front of the TV, battling over the remote control.

"It's *my* turn to choose the show!" hollered Sunil.

"No, it's *my* turn!" Vinnie shot back.

Uh-oh, Minka thought.

Just then – *sproing!*

The back of the remote flew off, and four small batteries *zinged* through the air.

Crack! One of the batteries hit the nail polish in Zoe's paw, shattering the glass bottle.

"No!" Zoe howled. "Ravenous Red is my *favourite!*"

Zip! Another battery knocked the needle right out of Penny Ling's paw.

"Oh, come on!" the panda groaned.

Bonk! The third battery bounced off Russell's head.

"Ow!" yelped the hedgehog.

Zoom! The fourth and final battery flew straight at Minka – but with a little quick thinking, she was able to grab it.

Zzzap! At that moment, the lights went out. The storm had knocked out the power, leaving seven pets in a dark room with nothing to do.

Everybody groaned at once – everybody except Minka.

Mrs Twombly poked her head through the curtain. "Goodness, that's a big storm out there!" she cried. "But I'm sure the power will be back on in no time. And Blythe will be here soon!"

All the pets adored Blythe Baxter – and she had a very special talent. Blythe could actually *understand* the animals when they spoke, instead of just hearing barks and growls and squawks and squeaks.

Minka turned to face her friends. "What's going on?" she asked. "Why are we letting a little rain ruin our day?"

"But Minka, there's nothing to *do*," replied Zoe. "It's raining too hard to go to the park…"

"And it's too dark to read…" added Russell.

"That doesn't mean we can't have fun!" Minka insisted.

But what could they do in a dark Day Camp while a tremendous thunderstorm raged outside?

Suddenly, inspiration struck.

"Glow tag!" Minka shrieked. "I have this great glow-in-the-dark paint, and it comes in loads of colours, so we can each have a colour to put on our hands – or, um, paws…"

"Or sticky webbed feet!" Vinnie spoke up.

"Or sticky webbed feet. Then we all run around in the dark and try to tag each other."

"Ooh, that sounds really fun!" exclaimed Pepper.

"But messy," Russell added.

"Don't worry about that," Minka reassured him. "We can wear our old T-shirts from the Petwalk Fundraiser last year, and play in the grooming station. Everybody, go and get your T-shirts!" Minka announced. "I'll grab my paints."

It wasn't easy to find everything they needed in the dark, but they were so eager to play glow tag that soon everybody was ready.

"Line up over here," Minka told her friends.

"Over where?" asked Vinnie.

"I can't see a thing!" Sunil said.

"Hang on, guys!" Russell announced. "I've got a torch."

Click! Just like that, the pets could see where they needed to stand.

Minka twirled a paintbrush. "Who's first?"

"I'll go!" Pepper exclaimed.

Minka pranced over to Pepper and painted some neon green paint on her paws.

"Done!" Minka announced. "Russell, turn off the torch for a second, would you?"

"Sure," Russell replied. Suddenly, the grooming station was pitch black – except for Pepper's glowing paws.

"Whoa! That's awesome!" Pepper exclaimed.

Working as quickly as she could, Minka painted each pet's paws a different colour.

"With glow tag, nobody's 'It'," Minka explained. "The goal is for everybody to tag as many pets as you can. On your mark – get set – go!"

Whoosh!

In a flash of neon colours, the pets zoomed off in all directions.

"Tag!" Minka shrieked, as she touched Pepper's shoulder.

"Oh!" Pepper exclaimed in surprise. "I didn't even see you coming!"

"That's the idea!" Minka replied, laughing so hard that she didn't even notice that Russell had crept up behind her until she felt him tap the tip of her tail. Now Minka was the only monkey in the whole wide world with a glow-in-the-dark tail!

The tile walls of the grooming station echoed with shrieks and laughter. Minka was having so much fun that she wished the game would never end. But then, without warning—

Zzzap!

The lights came back on. Everybody froze. Minka couldn't help giggling: everyone was splattered with a rainbow of glow-in-the-dark paint!

"It looks like you've been making the best of a stormy situation!" a voice said.

"Blythe!" Minka squealed. "When did you get here?"

"About ten minutes ago," Blythe replied. "Glow-in-the-dark tag – what an awesome idea. I can guess what's next on the agenda. Bath time! But first, I have big news."

The pets watched excitedly as Blythe took a deep breath. "I have received a very exciting invitation," she began. "I've been asked to design an exclusive line of clothing for the Endangered Animals Fund!"

All the pets broke into excited applause – even though they weren't all completely sure what this meant.

"There are a number of reasons why this is such a big deal," Blythe said. "First, it's a joint collection – for pets *and* people. You and your owner wearing matching outfits!"

"That would be just *fabulous!*" cried Zoe.

"And all the profits from sales of this collection will go to the Endangered

Animals Fund!" Blythe said. "The collection has to be stylish – but it also has to be different."

"Groundbreaking fashion is my very favourite kind!" Zoe gushed.

"That's good, because I'm going to need help," Blythe said. "This might just be one of the biggest opportunities ever, and I really don't want to blow it."

"Come on, you're the best designer ever!" Minka assured her. "You could never blow it."

"I guess not...now that I have my secret weapon," she replied.

"What's that?" asked Minka.

"You!" Blythe announced.

"M-me?" Minka echoed.

"Yes, you," Blythe said, smiling warmly.

"What if the fabrics for this exclusive new line featured your artwork?"

"Genius," Zoe breathed.

But Minka scrunched up her face in confusion. "Artwork on fabric?" she said. "How would that work? I paint on canvases."

"There's this really cool technology," Blythe explained. "You can paint on a canvas, like you always do. Then we'll ship your paintings to a special fabric manufacturer, and they'll make a custom fabric with your painting printed on it."

"They can do that?" Minka asked.

"They sure can. And if this works out, we could launch the first ever fashion line designed by pets and people for pets and people! What do you say, Minka? Will you do it?"

"Wow, Blythe!" Minka exclaimed. "*Of*

course I'll do it! But I'm going to need help. I really don't know much about fashion."

"Don't worry, Minka," Zoe assured her. "We'll set up some sort of fashion school for you and teach you everything you need to know. When I'm done, you'll know the difference between tweed and twill, bias binding and basting…"

"Basting? Like a turkey?" Vinnie asked, licking his lips.

"It's not the same thing at all!" Blythe said with a smile. "Basting is a way of temporary sewing, using big, long stitches that can easily be removed."

"That's a relief," joked Pepper. "Otherwise this new fashion line could get pretty sticky."

Minka joined in the laughter – but she was just as clueless as Vinnie. For the first time, Minka realised just how much she had to *learn* about fashion.

When Minka arrived at Day Camp the following morning, the weather was still grey and gloomy. Zoe, however, was as bright as a sunbeam as she met Minka at the entrance and led her to her favourite chair.

"Sit. Observe. Learn," Zoe ordered.

"Sit?" Minka asked, bouncing excitedly. "You know sitting's not exactly my strong suit!"

"Well, bounce around as much as you want – as long as you pay attention," Zoe replied.

"I know you've seen this before," Blythe began, as she held up her sketchbook.

"Sure I have," replied Minka, as

she whipped out her own, identical sketchbook. "I'd be lost without mine."

"So would I!" Blythe agreed. "But while you use yours for drawing all sorts of things, I use mine for fashion designs. "

Blythe opened her sketchbook and flipped to a page filled with sketches of adorable pet-sized hats.

"Ahh, last autumn's Blythe Style accessories collection," Zoe said in a dreamy voice. "One of my all-time favourites."

"Thanks," Blythe said. "So you see, Minka, every article of clothing starts with an idea – and a sketch is the first step to turn that idea into reality."

"Cool!" Minka said.

"Next up – patterns!" Zoe announced, as she carefully unfolded several pieces of tissue-thin paper.

"We use this special paper for all the parts of a particular piece of clothing and make adjustments until we get just the right fit," Blythe said.

"As you can imagine, a Great Dane needs a much bigger size than a pup," Zoe said.

"That's right, Zoe," Blythe said. "Then we use these pieces to cut the fabric before we sew it together."

"The fabric! That's practically my favourite part!" Zoe gushed.

"Sunil! Vinnie! You're up!" Blythe called.

There was a long silence while Minka, Blythe and Zoe waited. At last, Vinnie's voice echoed out from behind a screen. "Do we have to?" he asked.

"Yes, of course you do!" Zoe called back.

Minka heard a heavy sigh from behind the screen.

"Oh, fine," Vinnie finally said. "Come on, Sunil. Let's get it over with."

When Sunil and Vinnie shuffled out from behind the screen, Minka clapped her hands over her mouth. Sunil was wearing a sky-blue silk cape, covered in beads and frills, while Vinnie had a heavy wool cloak wrapped around his shoulders.

Sunil looked pained. "It's for a good cause," he muttered under his breath again and again.

"It absolutely is," Blythe assured him. "Thank you so much – both of you!"

Zoe straightened her shoulders and cleared her throat. "Now, Minka, I know these capes are a little…extreme," she began. "But Blythe whipped them up specially so you could see some fashion in action!"

Zoe launched into a long discussion about the differences between the capes. Minka tried to pay attention, but soon she was so busy making funny faces with Sunil and Vinnie that she was only half-listening to Zoe's lecture.

At last, Zoe finished, completely worn out. Sunil and Vinnie seized the opportunity to rip off their capes and scamper back into Day Camp.

"And *that* is pretty much everything I know about fashion," Zoe said. "Phew! That was exhausting."

Minka stifled a yawn. "It sure was."

A worried look crossed Zoe's face. "But it was useful, right?" she asked. "I mean, I hope it was."

"Oh, definitely," Minka assured her.

"I learned a lot about fashion." *At least, I learned a lot before I tuned out,* Minka thought with a twinge of guilt.

"Thank goodness!" Zoe said. "Because this new line is a very big deal. And it all starts with you!"

"Well, uh, I'll do my best," Minka replied. "I'd better get to work. There's no time like the present, right?"

"Yes!" cried Zoe. "Good luck, Minka! You can do it!"

But Minka had already disappeared into Day Camp. "Sketchbook… graphite…coloured pencils…" she muttered to herself as she looked for her art supplies.

Minka searched high and low, practically turning Day Camp inside out. She didn't find so much as a stubby crayon or smudgy eraser.

I know I'm not the neatest pet, she thought, *but how did I manage to lose all my art supplies since yesterday?*

That's when Minka realised something else: she was alone in Day Camp – and that was weirder than anything else.

"Blythe?" Minka called.

Click.

It was only the sound of a light switch being flipped on, but it was enough to make Minka jump. Someone was in Blythe's sewing room.

Blythe will know where everybody is, Minka thought. *Maybe she'll know where all my art stuff is, too!*

Minka was so excited she didn't just knock on the door – she nearly knocked it down. It swung open with a loud bang – and that's when Minka got the shock of her life.

"Surprise!" a chorus of voices yelled. With wide eyes, Minka saw Blythe and Zoe, Sunil and Vinnie, Pepper and Russell and Penny Ling all crowded together in Blythe's sewing room.

Read
Art from the Heart
to find out what happens next!